Can GRUNT the GRIZZLY Learn to Be Grateful?

Written by
Misty Black

Illustrated by
Ana Rankovic

PUNK AND FRIENDS

www.MistyBlackAuthor.com

Can Grunt the Grizzly Learn to Be Grateful
Formally *Grunt the Grizzly Learns to Be Grateful*
Punk and Friends Learn Social Skills series

Copyright © 2020 Berry Patch Press

For copyright permissions, school visits, and book readings/signings, email info@mistyblackauthor.com.

Written by Misty Black
Illustrated by Ana Rankovic
Edited by Shannon Jade

ISBN Paperback 978-1-951292-30-0
ISBN Hardback 978-1-951292-31-7
ISBN Audiobook 978-1-951292-63-8

Library of Congress Control Number: 2020948577

Published by Berry Patch Press, LLC. Clearfield, Utah.
First Edition 2020

www.MistyBlackAuthor.com

Dedicated to my husband and kids. I am forever GRATEFUL for your support and encouragement.

—Misty

Also available in Spanish:

¿Óscar el Oso aprenderá a ser agradecido?

Grunt the Grizzly was a GRUMPY bear.
He woke up grumpy. "My fur's a mess!"

He was grumpy during breakfast.
"These eggs are cold."

He was even grumpy during recess. "I don't like to lose!"

Grunt's grumpiness made him SAD!

"Good game." Punk the Skunk smiled.

Grunt glared. "Why are you so happy? We lost! Doesn't anything get you down?"

"Not normally," said Punk. "There's SO MUCH to be grateful for."

"Like what?" Grunt growled.

"I'm GRATEFUL I got my cast off. Now I can throw the ball better," Clutz the Cat said.

"I'm THANKFUL that I'm good at painting." Sloan the Sloth smiled.

"I'm BLESSED to have good friends," added Brave the Beaver.

"When a bad mood starts to creep in, we fight it off by saying,

Grumpies, grumpies, go away!
I would rather smile today.
When I'm grateful, I can see
all the good surrounding me.

Then we smile. Try it!" Punk said.

Grunt didn't feel like smiling, but he was tired of feeling GRUMPY.

He slowly lifted the left corner of his mouth.

That feels good, he thought.

He slowly lifted the right corner of his mouth.

Even better!

He stretched his GRIZZLY GRIN until his sparkly white teeth were beaming.

Grunt let out a chuckle . . .

. . . which made Punk and Clutz giggle.

Soon, everyone was laughing.

Grunt wanted the happy feeling to stay, so he took Punk's advice and looked for things to be grateful for.

Look at the colorful trees. The birds' songs are pretty. The air smells so fresh.

When Grunt **THANKED** his mom for cleaning their den, she looked up in surprise. "You're welcome."

That night, instead of whining about his hard bed, Grunt focused on his soft blanket. He fell asleep smiling.

But in the morning,
his smile faded.
"My fur's a mess!"
Grunt groaned.

**Then he stopped. Complaining wouldn't make him feel better.
Instead, he said,**

*"Grumpies, grumpies, go away!
I would rather smile today.
When I'm grateful, I can see
all the good surrounding me."*

"I'm grateful for warm baths and a brush," Grunt said.

Instead of complaining
about breakfast...

...he **THANKED** his parents for the meal, then left for school.

Before recess, Grunt thanked his friends for helping him see the good all around him.

But when they headed
outside to play soccer,
it started to pour.

"GRRRR! Rain ruins everything!"
Grunt complained.

The looks on his friends' faces reminded Grunt to look
on the BRIGHT SIDE of things.

Instead of letting the rain ruin his good mood, Grunt ran outside and began JUMPING and SPLASHING in puddles.

When his friends joined him, Grunt laughed. "This is way better than soccer!"

It was still pouring when the grizzly family sat down for dinner. Grunt looked at everyone's gloomy faces.

"I bet I can make you all SMILE!" Grunt grinned.

"What's there to smile about?" Grunt's dad huffed.

"Lots of things," Grunt said. "Like our safe den, our berry patch, and this delicious meal."

Then Grunt said,
"Grumpies, grumpies, go away!
I would rather smile today.
When I'm grateful, I can see
all the good surrounding me."

"Try it! Say something you're thankful for."

"I'm grateful for my teddy bear, Bella,"
said Grunt's sister.

"I'm thankful you're doing the dishes,"
Grunt's dad teased.

"I have an easy one." Grunt's mom smiled.
"I'M GRATEFUL FOR ..."

"You!" she said.

Grunt giggled. "And I'm grateful for

BIG
BEAR
HUGS!"

Let's Have a Discussion

When we're grateful, it helps us notice all the wonderful things around us. COUNTING OUR BLESSINGS is a very powerful tool for happiness.

Time yourself for one minute and start listing things you're grateful for out loud. How many things did you list?

Writing in a gratitude journal is one way to focus on the positive and be able to handle negative things and situations better.

Try writing three things you're grateful for here for the next three days and see if it helps you feel more joy.

Day 1   Day 2   Day 3

About the Author

Misty Black is a wife and mother of three amazing children. She believes gratitude plays a significant role in a happy life. She puts it best when she says, "Gratitude parts the storm clouds of life and allows sunshine to enter our souls." She and her family are much happier when they focus on the good and count their many blessings.

Grunt the Grizzly Learns to Be Grateful is the fifth book in the Punk and Friends series. It's Misty's tenth published children's book.

Misty enjoys reading, hiking, gardening, playing board games, camping, and spending time with family and friends.

Do you own a store, or are you looking for fundraising opportunities? Email info@mistyblackauthor.com for details on selling her books.

Grunt says,
"Don't forget to leave a review!"

**Follow Misty on social media @mistyblackauthor.
Join her VIP list for offers and promotions at**
www.MistyBlackAuthor.com

Would you like
AUTHOR
Misty
Black

to READ to
your school?

Ask your teacher or librarian to email her:
info@mistyblackauthor.com

Misty
Black
AUTHOR.COM

www.MistyBlackAuthor.com

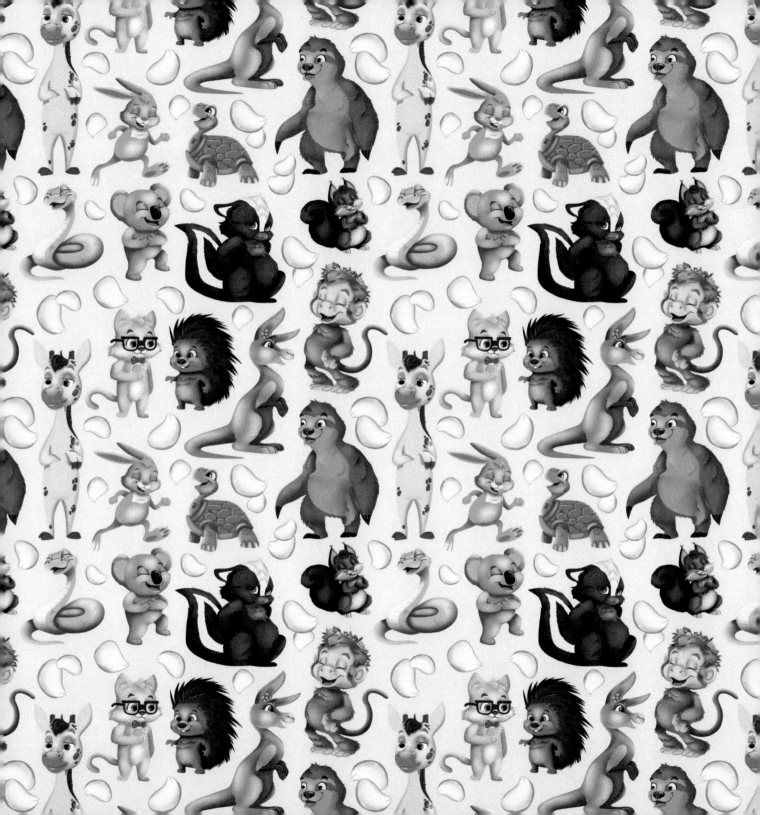

Made in the USA
Las Vegas, NV
22 August 2023

76418627R00021